WHO INVENTED
BASKETBALL?

JAMES NAISMITH

Sara L. Latta

Enslow Elementary
an imprint of
Enslow Publishers, Inc.

E 40 Industrial Road
Box 398
Berkeley Heights, NJ 07922
USA
http://www.enslow.com

CONTENTS

WORDS TO KNOW

dribble—To bounce a basketball on the floor.

inventor—A person who makes something new for the first time, or thinks of a better way to do something.

minister—A person whose job is to perform religious services.

university—A school that some people go to after they finish high school.

WHO INVENTED BASKETBALL?

James Naismith lived from 1861 to 1939.

Dribble, pass, and throw. Swish! The ball sails through the hoop. Score! Basketball is fun to watch. It is also fun to play. James Naismith invented the game of basketball in 1891.

A BOYHOOD IN
CANADA

James Naismith grew up in Canada. When he was eight years old, his father and mother died. Naismith, his brother, and sister went to live with their Uncle Peter. Naismith made many friends at his new home.

This is the house where Naismith grew up.

James, left, with his best friend, Robert McKenzie

MAKING HIS OWN
SKATES

Naismith and his friends loved to play games.
One time, Naismith watched his friends ice skate.

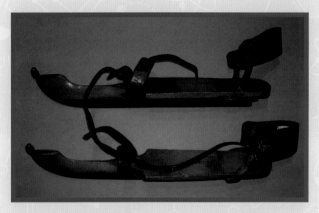

He did not have ice skates.
So he went to his uncle's
shop and made a pair.
Even as a boy, Naismith
was an **inventor**!

Naismith built wooden ice skates.
He put metal files on the bottom.

NAISMITH
STUDIES
TO BE A MINISTER

After finishing high school, Naismith went to school in Canada. He wanted to become a **minister**. He worked hard there. He played hard, too. He learned to play different games and sports.

Naismith loved playing sports. He was on the rugby team at McGill University.

NAISMITH
FINDS A
NEW JOB

Naismith got a job as a school minister. He also taught the young people how to play sports. The students could not play outdoors in the cold winter. They were bored. They got into trouble. Naismith's boss asked him to make up a game that the students could play indoors.

A NEW INDOOR GAME

Naismith put two wooden peach baskets high up on each end of a gym. Nine players on each team threw a ball to each other. They had to throw the ball into the basket at their end of the gym. If it stayed in the basket, they got three points.

The peach basket was soon replaced by a hoop with a net hanging below. In 1906, people decided to cut a hole in the net to let the ball fall through.

16

BASKET

BALL

Naismith's students played the first game of "Basket Ball" in December 1891. "It was the start of the first basketball game and the finish of trouble with that class," Naismith said. Soon, students at other schools wanted to play this new game.

Naismith sits with the first basketball team. He is the man in the blue suit.

NAISMITH MOVES TO
KANSAS

Naismith was not done learning. He became a doctor. In 1898, Naismith got a job at the **University** of Kansas. He started a basketball team there. Today, basketball is one of the best-loved games of all time. Thanks, Dr. Naismith!

A statue of James Naismith was unveiled in 2011 in his hometown, Almonte, Canada.

Naismith taught girls to play basketball too.
Here, he talks with the girls team at the
University of Kansas, around 1922.

ACTIVITY: PLAY DUCK ON A ROCK

When Naismith was a boy, he and his friends played a game called Duck on a Rock. This game gave him the idea for basketball. You can play Duck on a Rock, too!

You Will Need:

❖ A beanbag for each player
❖ A stool about as high as your waist.

What To Do:

1. Draw a line about ten feet from the stool. Each player stands behind the line and throws a beanbag toward the stool. The player whose beanbag lands nearest the stool is "it." That player places a beanbag, or "duck," on top of the stool. The "it" player stands near the stool.

2. One by one, the other players stand behind the line and throw their beanbags at the duck. If the player knocks the duck off the stool with a beanbag, he or she picks it up and goes to the back of the line. The "it" player places the duck back on the top of the stool.

James and his friends used this stone to play their favorite game, Duck on a Rock.

3. If the player throwing the beanbag does not knock the duck off the stool, he or she must pick up the beanbag and run past the throw line before getting tagged by "it." The player who is tagged then becomes "it" and places his or her own beanbag on top of the stool.

LEARN MORE

BOOKS

Gibbons, Gail. *My Basketball Book*. New York: HarperCollins, 2000.

Hareas, John. *Basketball*. New York: DK Children, 2005.

Miller, Amanda. *Let's Talk Basketball*. New York: Children's Press, 2008.

Ulmer, Michael. *J is for Jump Shot: A Basketball Alphabet*. Farmington Hills, Mich.: Sleeping Bear Press, 2005.

WEB SITES

Basketball Hall of Fame

   <http://www.hoophall.com>

History of Basketball

   <http://www.kansasheritage.org/people/naismith.html>

Naismith Museum and Hall of Fame

   <http://www.naismithmuseum.com>

INDEX

Enslow Elementary, an imprint of Enslow Publishers, Inc.

Enslow Elementary® is a registered trademark of Enslow Publishers, Inc.

Copyright © 2012 by Sara L. Latta

Library of Congress Cataloging-in-Publication Data

Latta, Sara L.
  Who invented basketball? James Naismith / Sara L. Latta.
    p. cm. — (I like inventors!)
  Includes index.
  Summary: "Find out about James Naismith—the man who invented basketball"—Provided by publisher.
  ISBN 978-0-7660-3965-0
  1. Naismith, James, 1861–1939—Juvenile literature.
  2. Basketball—United States—History—Juvenile literature.
  I. Title.
  GV884.N34L37 2013
  796.323092—dc22
  [B]
                                          2011014805

Future editions:
Paperback ISBN 978-1-4644-0131-2
ePUB ISBN 978-1-4645-1038-0
PDF ISBN 978-1-4646-1038-7

Printed in China
012012 Leo Paper Group, Heshan City, Guangdong, China

10 9 8 7 6 5 4 3 2 1

To Our Readers: We have done our best to make sure all Internet Addresses in this book w active and appropriate when we went to press. However, the author and the publisher have control over and assume no liability for the material available on those Internet sites or other Web sites they may link to. Any comments or suggestions can be sent by e-mail comments@enslow.com or to the address on the back cover.

Series Consultant:
Duncan R. Jamieson, PhD
Professor of History
Ashland University
Ashland, OH

Series Literacy Consultant:
Allan A. De Fina, PhD
Dean, College of Education
Professor of Literacy Education
New Jersey City University
Past President of the New Jersey Reading Association

Photo Credits: © 1999 Artville, LLC, p. 6; The Dr. James Naismith Museum, p. 14; Courtesy of Springfield College, Babson Library, Archives and Special, p. 16; The Dr. Jar Naismith Museum, pp. 8, 9, 15 (inset), 21; The Estate of Willard Mullin, Shirley Mullin Rhodes, p. 12; Kansas State Historical Society, pp. 5 (photograph has been color-enhance 19; Library of Congress, Prints and Photographs, p. 17; McGill University Archives, Photographic Collection, PL 007415, pp. 11, 13; Michael Dunn, pp. 7, 18; Petur Asgeirss Shutterstock.com, p. 3 (dribble); Shutterstock.com, pp. 1, 2, 3 (inventor, minister, university), 4, 15, 22, 23.

Cover Photo: Shutterstock.com; Kansas State Historical Society (inset; photograph has be color-enhanced).